THIS Picture Knight BOOK
BELONGS TO

....

The Adventures of Maurice Mini Minor

GEOFFREY BAKER

Maurice
cools things down

illustrated by Rolf Harris

Picture Knight

HODDER AND STOUGHTON

For Grimoldby County Primary School

From an original idea by Dr P. Mansfield and Terry Moule

British Library Cataloguing in Publication Data

Baker, Geoffrey
Maurice cools things down.
I. Title   II. Harris, Rolf, *1930-*   III. Series
823'.914 [J]

ISBN 0-340-52957-1

First published 1990 by Picture Knight

Published by Hodder and Stoughton Children's Books,
a division of Hodder and Stoughton Ltd,
Mill Road, Dunton Green, Sevenoaks, Kent TN13 2YA
Editorial office: 47 Bedford Square, London WC1E 7DP

Printed in Great Britain by Cambus Litho, East Kilbride

'Wonderful!' said Maurice Mini Minor. He had just got rid of all his stale, old oil and filled up with fresh, pure oil at Mr Lovely's Excellent Garage. Sir Reginald Hoy-Titoyty was waiting for him. They were going on an adventure.

'Upwards and onwards,' boomed Sir Reginald.

Just then, Cheeky Beetle drove by and hooted loudly. 'Listen everybody,' he shouted. 'Naples is down in the dumps, down in the car park. Follow me.'

'That sounds like one of your silly jokes,' said Maurice firmly. 'Naples is never down in the dumps.'

'It's not a joke, honest,' said Cheeky Beetle.

'Come on then,' said Maurice with a sigh, 'let's see.'

'If we are on a wild goose chase,' said Sir Reginald, 'we are not amused.'

When they reached the car park, Naples, who normally roared about madly, really *was* looking miserable.

'What's got into you?' cried Maurice.

'Something has,' moaned Naples. 'My temperature gauge is shooting up and my engine is racing too fast and I'm shaking.'

'Well don't get too hot,' said Maurice. 'Just keep your scarf round you and stand in the shade. It's probably nothing.'

'I know,' said Cheeky Beetle, 'let's play Naples' favourite game. That will cheer him up.'

'Cricket,' thundered Sir Reginald. 'Splendid!'

'Not *cricket*,' yelled Cheeky Beetle. 'Hide-and-seek of course.'

'Shall we try?' asked Maurice.

'I suppose so,' said Naples quietly.

'I'll be *it*,' shouted Cheeky Beetle. 'One – two – three – a hundred.'

'Hold your horses,' boomed Sir Reginald. 'We haven't even started.'

'Just a joke,' laughed Cheeky Beetle. 'Off you go.'

Maurice hid behind the ticket machine. Sir Reginald tried to hide behind a flag pole with a Union Jack flying from it.

Naples stood quietly in the shade behind
a big bin full of empty bottles.

'Ninety-eight, ninety-nine, a hundred! I'm coming!' shouted Cheeky Beetle. He saw Sir Reginald straight away. 'Found you,' he cried.

'Anyway, I wasn't made for hiding away,' muttered Sir Reginald.

'Come on,' yelled Cheeky Beetle, 'we have to find the others.'

'Wait!' exclaimed Sir Reginald, 'I've just remembered something. We didn't get tickets for the car park!'

He drove straight to the machine. 'Don't worry, I'll treat you,' he boomed.

Maurice stayed very still behind the machine and then he squeaked in a funny voice, 'Thunder ... and ... lightning.'

'Thunder and lightning!' bellowed Sir Reginald, 'the thing talked ... take cover!'

'It's only me, Sir Reginald,' Maurice laughed, poking his bonnet out from behind the ticket machine.

'I knew it was you all the time,' muttered Sir Reginald.

'Found you, Maurice,' yelled Cheeky Beetle.

'Now we must find Naples,' Maurice said. 'I wonder where he could be?'

They began to search. Then Cheeky Beetle cried, 'Look!'

From behind the bin of empty bottles rose a puff of steam and then a bigger one and then a really big one, rising up into the air like a white cloud.

'Naples!' they all cried and drove quickly to him.

A fountain of steamy, hot water was shooting out of Naples' radiator and dripping down all over him.

'Well,' said Maurice, 'he's got a fever. Something's not quite right.'

'I'm so hot,' Naples cried.

'Put a stopper in it,' yelled Cheeky Beetle.

'Shivering chassis!' exclaimed Maurice. 'Don't do that! Never try to stop a fever; it's helping you.'

'Ooooh,' groaned Naples.

'Right everyone,' said Maurice, 'let's see if we can spot what Naples' problem is.'

They all stared at poor Naples who moaned and groaned until all the steam had drifted away. Then he sighed a very big sigh and said, 'Oh, I do feel so thirsty. I wish I were in Venice.'

'There's the trouble,' Maurice announced. 'Look on the ground.' There, lying in tatters and shreds, was Naples' fan-belt.

'Don't worry,' said Maurice, 'we will soon get a new one fitted and I will get you a big can of fresh water from Mr Lovely's Excellent Garage too. Then, provided you drink it slowly with your engine ticking over gently, you'll soon be roaring round again.'

'Here, here,' boomed Sir Reginald.

'Who won the hide-and-seek?' asked Naples with a hint of a smile.

'Why *you* did of course,' they all cried, and Maurice sang a little song as he drove off to get the water for his friend.

Poor old Naples, normally noisy,
Quietly stood alone,
He'd come to play his favourite game
But wished he had stayed at home.
His temperature was rising,
He hardly made a sound,
'I can't, I can't, I can't,' he moaned,
'I just can't roar around.'

'Don't worry at all,' we shouted,
'Before you can count to ten,
With fan-belt mended,
And new cool water,
You'll roar around again.'

So
If you're hottish and floppish and really weak

And you're feeling too ill to play hide-and-seek,
If you're under the covers and everything
  aches,
And you want to lie still but you can't stop
  the shakes;
If you think of your friends in the park having
  fun,
And all you can do is feel hot as the sun;
If you're tossing and turning and dripping
  with heat
From the tip of your nose to the toes on your
  feet;
Remember how Naples got wetter and
  wetter,
This silly old fever is making you better.

I sing this song as I drive along,
Maurice Mini Minor;
I get there soon 'cause I keep in tune,
Maurice Mini Minor;
And when you see me passing by,
Just toot your horn and wink your eye,
No need to wonder who am I,
Maurice Mini Minor.